BILLY SURE
KID ENTREPRENEUR

vs. MANNY REYES
KID ENTREPRENEUR

INVENTED BY **LUKE SHARPE**
DRAWINGS BY **GRAHAM ROSS**

THE CANDY TOOTHBRUSH

WITHDRAWN

Simon Spotlight

New York London Toronto Sydney New Delhi

SIMON SPOTLIGHT

An imprint of Simon & Schuster Children's Publishing Division

1230 Avenue of the Americas, New York, New York 10020

This Simon Spotlight paperback edition February 2017

Copyright © 2017 by Simon & Schuster, Inc. Text by Michael Teitelbaum.

Illustrations by Graham Ross. All rights reserved, including the right of reproduction in whole or in part in any form.

SIMON SPOTLIGHT and colophon are registered trademarks of Simon & Schuster, Inc.

For information about special discounts for bulk purchases, please contact Simon & Schuster Special Sales at 1-866-506-1949 or business@simonandschuster.com.

Designed by Jay Colvin

The text of this book was set in Minya Nouvelle.

Manufactured in the United States of America 0117 OFF

10 9 8 7 6 5 4 3 2 1

ISBN 978-1-4814-7907-3 (hc)

ISBN 978-1-4814-7906-6 (pbk)

ISBN 978-1-4814-7908-0 (eBook)

Library of Congress Catalog Card Number 2016940850

Chapter One

Summer Vacation in the Sandbox

MY NAME IS BILLY SURE. AS OF TODAY, I CAN officially say I am no longer a seventh-grader at Fillmore Middle School. No, I'm not moving—though my family *almost* moved to Italy not too long ago (long story). I can say that because I'm now an *eighth*-grader at Fillmore Middle School!

Well, as my sister Emily might tell you, I'm not technically an eighth-grader yet, because it's still the summer *before* eighth grade, but I'm going to go ahead and call myself that anyway. You've got to celebrate the small things, right?

Anyway, it feels like just yesterday was the first day of seventh grade, when I went back to school after my first invention, the ALL BALL,

went on sale. For as long as I can remember, I have always been coming up with invention ideas. It used to be a hobby, but together with my best friend Manny, we founded an invention company—SURE THINGS, INC. I am the CEO and do the inventing, and Manny is the CFO, or Chief Financial Officer, and does the marketing, sales, and a whole lot of other cool stuff I don't really understand. That's how it's always been, and how it's always going to be!

Still, it's kind of crazy to think it's been almost a year since Sure Things, Inc. started. And it's also kind of crazy to think that today, summer vacation has started! Which means I can spend my days relaxing, taking my dog Philo on long walks, and, oh yeah, being a normal thirteen-year-old kid.

Just as I'm thinking about all of this, **Ping!** there's a notification on my laptop screen. I have an important e-mail to read.

Oh no, I think. *I hope everything is okay with the Everything Locator.* The EVERYTHING LOCATOR is Sure Things, Inc.'s newest invention, and I think it's going to be our biggest hit yet.

I sign into my account and brace myself. But *phew*. The notification wasn't from Manny saying that our invention is doomed. It's from the makers of *Sandbox XXL*, only the very best video game in the world!

Dear Billy Sure,
Congratulations! You are now officially set up with a player account for *Sandbox XXL*, everyone's favorite action-packed adventure. Please download the game at the link below. Have fun, and remember, in this game it's good to have your head in the sand!

Remember when I said I want to be a normal thirteen-year-old kid? Well, scratch that! I'm not a normal thirteen-year-old kid—I'm a thirteen-year-old kid with access to *Sandbox XXL*! YES!

I've been on this video game's wait list for months, and I can't believe it's finally my time to play.

Just as I download it and the game starts to install, I hear a voice from outside my door.

"Billy!" says the voice.

That's my mom.

"Billy, have you finished unpacking?" Mom asks, peeking into my room.

I groan. Yeah, unpacking. Remember when I said that my family almost moved to Italy? Well, we cut it pretty close. My dad is an artist, and he was offered a job to do a series of paintings at a gallery over there. We had everything packed and ready to go—until Manny and I discovered that the art commissioner wasn't a real art commissioner, she was actually the CEO of our rival invention company, Nat

Definite, and it was all a ruse to get me out of the inventing biz! Thankfully we made a deal with her—she still had to commission Dad for some art, but he could do it right here at home. Case closed, right?

Not so much. Because thanks to Nat's alter ego, "Tali DeCiso," I now have a huge chore ahead of me—unpacking.

"I'll start that now, Mom," I say, looking sadly at my computer screen. How can my inventing rival still be messing up my life?

I spend some time emptying the last few boxes and put stuff back where it belongs. My dog, Philo, curls up on a pile of stinky socks that I unpack. I'm not sure why the socks are stinky and I definitely don't understand why Philo wants to sleep on them. *Thanks for all the help, Philo,* I think.

I go throughout the house putting things back, like my bathroom towels in the bathroom.

In the kitchen I see Dad's artist's lamp sitting on the counter in the exact spot where the blender should be. *So what's in Dad's art studio?* I think.

Curiosity gets the better of me and I head out of the house to his art studio, which is conveniently located in the garden shed.

Aha! Neatly poised above Dad's drawing board is the missing blender!

I guess Dad got a bit confused while he was unpacking, I think.

I head into the house and back up to my room. As I pass the bathroom I see a spatula sitting in the toothbrush holder.

Oh no, I think, realizing Dad made breakfast earlier today. *What did he use to cook with?*

Finally, after an hour of unpacking, I settle down in front of my computer and enter the world of *Sandbox XXL!*

The game starts off simply enough. I get to create my avatar, which of course looks just like me only . . . *Sandbox XXL*-like.

I build my house—which looks a lot like a medieval castle—and walk around until I run into a GIANT SAND MONSTER who charges right at me!!!

I race to the water and dive into the ocean. Knowing he will be instantly dissolved if he follows, the sand monster roars in anger, waving his dusty fist at me. Unfortunately, I know that the game won't let me stay in the ocean forever. After a few more seconds a giant wave approaches from behind.

If I stay in the water I'll get crushed by the wave. If I go back out onto the beach, the sand monster will get me. There's only one thing to do. I must control the huge wave of water and direct it onto the sand monster.

Just a video game, I remind myself. *Nothing to be afraid of.*

I start using the arrow keys on my keyboard, and I don't think my reflexes have worked this fast *ever.* Up, down, up, left, left, across, side—

I hardly notice the time, but suddenly two hours have passed.

"Billy! Dinnertime!" Dad calls.

"I'm not hungry," I call back, pausing the game midbattle. I don't even want to imagine what toothbrush-infested food Dad has managed to cook up.

Then I hear my mom's voice.

"It's Chinese takeout," she calls.

CHINESE TAKEOUT? Well, that's an eggroll of a different color. There are very few things more important than defeating a giant sand monster. Chinese takeout is one of them!

Leaving the game paused, I scramble downstairs. On my way to the kitchen I pass through the living room and see that the vacuum cleaner is sitting on the TV stand. I wonder where the TV could be?

Shrugging, I head to the kitchen and take a seat. Boxes of Chinese food are spread out across the table. I grab the biggest box, dump a huge helping of lo mein onto my plate, and start shoveling noodles into my mouth.

"I have to admit, I'm glad we didn't move to Italy," says Mom, pouring some wonton soup into a bowl. "Lots of lasagna, but we would have missed the food from here!"

I nod and moan my agreement, lo mein dangling from my mouth. Everyone looks at my older sister Emily, waiting for her to comment—something that is always unpredictable—but she says nothing.

"And I am COMPLETELY UNPACKED!" Dad says proudly, dumping a pile of fried rice onto his plate.

I wonder if he knows just how bad of a job he did with the unpacking.

I reach in to grab an egg roll. That's when I realize that not only is Emily quiet, but she also hasn't had a single bite of food or even taken any to eat. Her plate is completely clean.

Of course, the less Emily eats, the more there is for me, but it's still weird since Emily *loves* Chinese food. She sits at the other end of the table, arms crossed in front of her. I wonder what she's grumpy about today.

"Come on, Em, at least try the lo mein," Mom says. "The noodles are soft."

Emily grunts but remains tight-lipped.

Maybe this is just Emily's latest "thing," I think. My sister is known for her "things." Let's see . . . some of Emily's things have included wearing glasses without lenses, speaking only in a British accent, painting each of her fingernails different colors, and her latest (before whatever this one is now)—using random Italian words incorrectly when she thought we were all moving to Italy.

After my fourth helping of lo mein, I'm full. I help clear the table. When I'm done, I head upstairs to resume my game. It's time for level two where I'll have to defeat the EVIL SUPER SAND FLY STORM!

Chapter Two

From the Sandbox to the Office

A HUGE WAVE SLAMS ME IN THE BACK OF THE head, knocking me down into the ocean. I'm completely underwater, yet somehow I can still breathe. A colorful tropical fish swims by and I pause to admire its beauty.

Just as I'm doing that, the fish turns into a shark. It races toward me with its mouth wide open!

Sandbox XXL! I think. I'm just playing *Sandbox XXL.* The shark is not real.

But wait! *I'm* in the game . . . not my avatar. And *I'm* about to be devoured by the shark!

I swim as fast I can away from the shark and back to the beach, which is when a giant sand monster sends me back into the water!

I'm going down . . . down . . . down. . . .

Until another colorful fish swims up to me and says, "It's only a game, after all."

A talking fish?! Something is wrong here.

And that's when I wake up.

I sit up in bed and discover that I'm still dressed in the clothes I wore yesterday. Next to my pillow is my laptop, with *Sandbox XXL* on the screen. The theme music is still playing.

Okay, I know I only started yesterday, but I think it's already time for me to put the game away for a while.

I quickly shower, feed Philo, and grab some breakfast.

"Wanna go for a walk, buddy?" I ask Philo as he finishes his breakfast and licks the bowl clean.

Philo's ears perk up at the word "walk," and he scampers to the front door.

I head outside, hop on my bike, and take

off on a morning ride. Philo trots beside me. I start to daydream . . . and wonder what would happen if right now a three-headed sand monster showed up!

Yeah . . . I've definitely been playing a little too much *Sandbox XXL*.

As we continue our walk, **Ding!** I get an incoming text from Manny.

HQ today?

I glance at Philo, who has just finished his business, and text back:

K. See ya in a few!

I stop at home for a brief second to tell Mom where I'll be and grab my laptop. Then I ride my bike to the World Headquarters of Sure Things, Inc.—also known as Manny's garage.

When I get there, I hop off my bike and head inside. Philo follows me and immediately curls up in his doggy bed—just another day at the office for Philo.

"Thanks for stopping by, Billy," says Manny. Then he gets right down to business. "I've reviewed the sales figures for all our inventions this year so far, and came up with some pretty cool marketing strategies for *all* of our products, not just the new stuff. I'm talking about the ALL BALL, the SIBLING SILENCER, and all the others. We need to revamp our efforts across the board. You know, to remind people where it all started for Sure Things, Inc."

That's my friend Manny. I love his dedication, though sometimes I worry that he works too hard and doesn't have enough fun. Just don't tell him I think that!

"That all sounds great. But what do you need me for?" I ask.

"Well, I'm thinking this marketing strategy would be best launched alongside a new product," Manny begins.

Uh-oh, I know where this is going . . .

"So, even though it's summer vacation, I think we should start working on our Next Big Thing," says Manny, like coming up with a new invention is no big deal.

I grimace.

"I'm not really ready yet, Manny," I say, figuring he'll certainly understand. "I mean, you know how much I love inventing, but I don't want to feel pressured. We both worked really hard all school year, not to mention everything that's happened with Sure Things, Inc. I just want to chill. Play some *Sandbox XXL*, ride my bike, you know. Just for a little bit."

This isn't the first time I've wanted to relax. But come on. This is *summer vacation* we are talking about!

Manny frowns, something he doesn't usually do.

"Billy, we can't just stop inventing over summer break. We're an invention company. That's what we do. We don't loaf around on the beach. We invent." Manny shakes his head and continues. "A company needs new products all the time. That's what being in business means. Customers and retailers have short memories. If we wait too long, we'll lose valuable retail space to other companies. And once that happens we may never get it back."

I don't know what to say. Manny knows a lot more about business than I do, so he's probably right about all this.

But also I really want a summer vacation. "Okay, Manny, just let me finish this level and then we'll talk about a new invention." I pull out my phone and start playing the mobile version of *Sandbox XXL*.

But Manny isn't done yet.

"Billy, what's the point of playing that video game?" he asks. "Or any video game, really? Why *pretend* that you're doing something exciting when you can actually *do* something exciting, like invent a new product?"

A tense silence fills the room. I try to focus on my game, but I feel Manny staring at me.

"C'mon, partner," Manny says, breaking

the silence. "Can't we think of something together? It's what we always do."

I hear what Manny says, but I ignore him. Partly because I'm a little annoyed at how insistent he is. It's like he's not listening to what I have to say. And partly because I'm locked into *Sandbox XXL* again, where I'm about to roll a giant ball of wet sand over an army of RADIOACTIVE CRABS. If I can destroy the creatures in the next ten seconds, I'll advance to the next level.

I steer the sloppy ball of sand toward the glowing red crabs, but they're cleverer than I thought. They form lines and start crawling in a bunch of different directions. My wet sand ball rolls right past them.

I want to make it to the next level, and I also really don't want to be having this conversation with Manny right now. As I plan my next attack against the crabs, **KER-BLAM!** A brilliant idea pops into my head!

"Why don't *you* invent something, partner?" I say, anxious to remain focused on the game. "Instead of staring at your spreadsheets all day?"

The running-out-of-time music starts playing. . . .

Within seconds, I'm surrounded. Mutant radioactive crabs rush at me from all sides. There's only one way out of this . . . and I take it. I dive into the water and begin my warrior's magic chant:

Ocean power within my hand, unleash your fury upon the sand!

A huge wave rises up, crashes onto the beach, and pulls all the radioactive crabs into the ocean.

Bing-boong! the game rings out, indicating that I have advanced to the next level. I turn to Manny. And that's when it hits me.

Did I just tell Manny to INVENT?!

"All right," Manny replies calmly. "Maybe I will. Maybe you'll have to start calling me Manny Reyes, Kid Entrepreneur!"

He's not done yet.

"Actually, I think it's a great idea," he continues. "And you, Billy, can manage the business side, since you *also* enjoy staring at screens all day." He points to the screen on my phone, where GIANT JELLYFISH are starting to plan an attack against my avatar.

Manny is smiling, but I feel bad.

I can't believe I was so short with Manny. I really didn't mean to be, I think.

"Manny, I'm sorry," I say, putting my phone down. "I didn't mean to be so snappy with you. I was just so locked into the game."

Manny shrugs. "No, I'm not upset," he says. "I actually think that us switching roles is a pretty good idea. That way we can understand what we each do a little better. It can be a competition, a friendly switcheroo! You'll get to see what I do up close, and vice versa. Actually, I think it could be healthy for the company."

I wasn't really being serious when I said that Manny should invent something, but when Manny puts it that way, it actually *might* be a good idea.

And how hard can it be? Sure, Manny is a marketing and business genius, but marketing and selling a product can't be as tough as, I don't know, inventing one from nothing, right?

"Okay!" I say. "You're on! What invention will you be working on? Maybe you can invent a video game that kids can play while also letting them pay attention to other people."

(I really do feel bad about snapping at Manny.)

Manny smiles, letting me know that he realizes how terrible I feel. Reason #913 why

I'm glad Manny is my best friend—we just get each other.

"Actually, I do have an idea for an invention," Manny says, turning serious.

"Already?" I ask, a bit shocked and a little jealous that Manny is able to come up with something so fast.

"Yup," Manny says. "And you're the one who inspired it. For my first invention as Manny Reyes, Kid Entrepreneur, I'm going to invent the CANDY TOOTHBRUSH!"

Chapter Three

Switcheroo!

I HAVE TO ADMIT, I DID *NOT* SEE THAT ONE COMING. It only took Manny about a second to come up with an idea for an invention—though technically we came up with it together years ago, when we were little kids.

Back when I first started inventing, I worked in a small corner of my bedroom that I turned into a workshop. And the first idea I tried to invent was the Candy Toothbrush. So many kids get fussy when it's time to brush their teeth that I thought if I could invent a tooth-brush that makes any toothpaste taste like candy (without causing cavities, of course), kids would love brushing their teeth. But I never could perfect it.

How will I feel if Manny can invent what I couldn't?

"What do you think, Billy?" Manny asks. "I like the Candy Toothbrush because it's a simple idea that kids will want to use and parents will be happy about. Makes your CFO job a bit easier, since it's an EASY SELL!"

Hmm . . . Manny does have a point. And it would be really nice for my first invention idea to actually see the light of day, even if I'm not the one inventing it.

"I think it's great, Manny!" I say, a little too enthusiastically. "I can't wait to see what you come up with."

I pick up my phone and am about to resume playing *Sandbox XXL* when Manny shoots me a puzzled glance.

"What are you doing?" he asks.

"I'm going to play some more *Sandbox XXL* while you invent the Candy Toothbrush," I reply. "Why? Should I be doing something else?"

"Have I ever waited until you were completely finished inventing something before I started selling it?" Manny asks.

Eek . . . aaaaagh.

Manny's right. I should have known that. In fact, there have been many times that Manny's habit of selling something I haven't invented yet has made me pretty nervous.

"Hmm," I say, putting down my phone. "So how are we going to make this role-switching thing work?"

"Well, I figure I'll sit at your workbench and try to figure out how to make the Candy Toothbrush," Manny explains. "I think you should start calling stores to check out interest in this new invention."

"Sounds okay to me," I say.

After all, how hard could this be?

Manny walks across the office and settles in at my workbench. I sit down at his desk and notice a line of files. They are sitting neatly in a file holder and each one has a colored-coded label: NEW INVENTIONS, INVENTIONS IN PROGRESS, MARKETING STRATEGIES FOR ALMOST-INVENTED IDEAS, and SALES RESULTS BY ZIP CODE.

Wow, Manny is one organized dude. But, then again, so am I—in my own special way.

I smile to myself, thinking what Manny says whenever he sees the, um, "organization" at my workbench.

Then I start to think about what kind of stores might be interested in carrying the Candy Toothbrush.

Let's see. I could call candy stores—that's a no-brainer. Also, convenience stores. I think that's where most people buy toothbrushes. Dentist offices. My dentist is always giving me a new toothbrush after a checkup.

Hmm. But what about stores that sell candy but aren't *just* candy stores? Would they be interested? Like supermarkets?

Maybe this sales thing isn't as straightforward as I thought. Manny always just jumps right into this part, like he has plans fully formed the minute I mention a new invention idea. I always like to joke about Manny selling things I haven't invented yet. But now that the tables are turned, it's no joke at all.

I always thought that the pressure was all on the inventor to create something that didn't exist. But I can see now that there's pressure on both sides.

I turn around just as Manny does the same.

"Getting started is tough," we both say in unison.

We laugh. At least I'm not the only one having trouble.

Philo looks up from his bed. He glances over at Manny sitting at my workbench. Then he looks over at me sitting at Manny's computer. Then he looks back at Manny, then me, then Manny.

Poor Philo must be really confused. He's so used to seeing us in our own workspaces. He whines, then decides that the best course of action is to put his head back down and continue his nap.

I wonder what it would be like to switch places with Philo, I think.

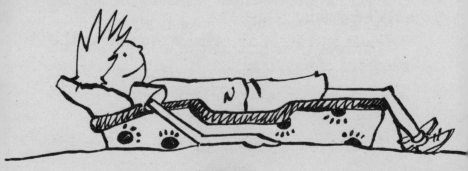

But since I haven't switched places with Philo, and I have with Manny, I start searching for candy stores. The first one that comes up is Sweet Tooth. Of course! I used to go there all the time when I was younger.

I dial the number and wait. Time to start my new career as a salesperson!

After two rings a woman answers.

"Hello! This is Sweet Tooth, where we satisfy your . . . *sweet tooth!* May I help you?" she says.

"Hi," I begin, trying not to let my nerves come through. "My name is Billy and I'm calling about a product I have coming out soon called the Candy Toothbrush. I think it would be perfect for your store."

Ooh, I like that last part. Maybe I do have a flair for this.

"Hold on a second," says the woman on the other end of the line.

I hear a click, followed by a really sappy version of a song that I think Mom likes.

Well, I think, *this isn't so hard.* In fact, the

hardest part so far has been having to listen to this horrible music! All I have to do now is wait for the person who answered the phone to get the right person for me to talk to. I may be making my first sale on my very first call.

A minute goes by. Then two. Then five.

After what feels like an hour, I realize that the terrible music isn't playing anymore. In fact, there is nothing happening on the other end of the phone.

Wait, did she hang up on me?

SHE TOTALLY HUNG UP ON ME! Before I even got to tell her why the Candy Toothbrush is so great!

Okay, so maybe I'm not the best salesperson after all.

Maybe just calling someone out of the blue isn't the best idea. Maybe I need to go to the store and talk to someone in person. Hmm. I can do that!

"Manny, I've got a sales meeting to make," I say, trying to sound as official and professional as possible. "I'll be back in a little bit."

As I head to the door, Philo gets up from his bed and stretches. He thinks we're going home.

"Stay, boy!" I say, pointing at his bed. "Stay here with Manny."

Philo lies back down.

As I pass my workbench on the way out, I see that Manny has glued half an old toothbrush to a small flashlight, both of which are covered in sticky blue goo.

I shake my head and leave. I hope I'm better at selling than Manny is at inventing.

I bike over to Sweet Tooth, where I discover, to my surprise, the place has been remodeled! The store looks like the inside of someone's mouth!

The walls are painted pinkish-red, and a giant gummy tongue runs down the middle of the floor. Some of the customers step onto

the squishy tongue. They say things like, "ooh, gross," and step right off. Others tromp around and laugh.

Jars filled with marshmallows hang down from the ceiling and pop up from the floor. They look like upper and lower teeth.

This is awesome! Not to mention, a store with marshmallows that look like teeth is the *perfect* place to sell the Candy Toothbrush. This should be a no-brainer (literally, since I don't see any candy brains in this store).

I head toward the main counter and pass a display featuring the FUNNY GUMMY. The Funny Gummy is the product that Dad designed the packaging for—the one released by Sure Things, Inc.'s rival company, Definite Devices. The Funny Gummy makes you crack jokes for nine minutes straight. Clearly this store likes inventive products.

I walk up to the counter and smile at the woman behind it.

"Hi there," I say. "I tried calling earlier. My name is Billy. I . . ."

As I'm talking, I notice that the woman is glaring at me, like I just insulted her.

Then it dawns on me. This must be the woman who hung up on me. She seems annoyed that I decided to follow up by actually coming in.

Got to press on, I tell myself. What would Manny say? *Trust the product.*

"I . . . um, well, actually, me—no, my company has a great new product coming out soon," I mumble, but keep going. "I think . . . *we* think, that it would be a great fit here in your store."

The woman says nothing and continues to stare at me like I just told her that I hate PUPPIES and RAINBOWS and SUMMER VACATION.

"Our new product fits right in with the theme you have here in your store. It's called the Candy Toothbrush."

I wait for some reaction. I'm not expecting her to give me a hug and instantly write me a big fat check, but I'm expecting some response to my sales pitch . . . you know, *any* response!

But nope. She remains silent and continues to stare at me.

"Let me explain exactly what the Candy Toothbrush will do," I continue, pretending she's responded as warmly as Philo does when I say anything that rhymes with "treat." "First, it—"

"BILLY SURE?!" squeals a high-pitched voice, cutting through the air.

Oh no. I'd recognize that voice anywhere. *Why now?* I think.

The voice belongs to Samantha Jenkins, a girl at my school. She's been one of my biggest fans ever since the All Ball. She was one of the first kids at school to join the Fillmore Inventors Club back when I started it. At first I thought she was kind of annoying, but I've grown to like her—when she's not yelling at me in candy shops, I mean!

As if to make matters worse, Samantha comes up next to me, and I see someone else walking next to her. It's her mother, Kathy

Jenkins, a reporter for the *Right Next Door* website. Kathy has published some unflattering and even untrue articles about me, Manny, and Sure Things, Inc.

"So, Billy," Kathy Jenkins says, taking her pen out of her pocket. "I couldn't help but overhear. Sure Things, Inc. has a new product that you think will do well at Sweet Tooth?"

Chapter Four

Billy Sure, Kid Salesperson?

I START TO ANSWER, BUT THIS TIME IT'S SOMEONE else's turn to interrupt me—the woman at the candy counter. The same woman who previously stared at me silently!

"Sure Things, Inc.?" she says.

I look over at her and see that her entire expression has changed. Instead of contempt and annoyance, it almost looks like she's interested!

What alternate universe am I living in?!

I nod and smile back at her.

"Well, why didn't you say so in the first

place? You must be the new Manny. My name is Claudia. Come on, let's talk business!" she says, and gestures for me to follow her.

I take a step to follow Claudia into her office, but Kathy Jenkins motions to me first. She leans in close, her eyes narrowing as she stares at me, like a sand dragon that has just spotted its prey—okay, okay, I'm super obsessed with *Sandbox XXL*, I know.

"The new Manny?" Kathy whispers.

I gulp. This kind of thing could be all kinds of bad depending how Kathy Jenkins spins the news story.

"It's no big deal," I say. "Manny and I are just doing a kind of switcheroo thing for a while. Just an experiment. Anyway, I gotta go. See ya! Bye, Samantha!"

As I hurry toward Claudia's office, I can feel Kathy's eyes burn a hole in the back of my head.

I settle into a chair in Claudia's office.

"I'm the owner of Sweet Tooth," she begins. "So, tell me all about the newest Sure Thing!" She smiles and raises her eyebrows, like she's the first person to ever make this joke.

I am amazed at the complete turnaround Claudia has done, from wishing I would just VANISH INTO THE FLOORBOARDS to inviting me into her office the second that Sure Things, Inc. was mentioned.

So, lesson learned. The power of the Sure Things, Inc. brand puts me in a whole different category than if I was just some kid who walked in off the street to try to sell something.

All right. *Now* this is going to be easy! For real!

"Our newest idea is called the Candy Toothbrush," I begin. I feel confident.

"Basically, the Candy Toothbrush is a special toothbrush that takes any kind of toothpaste and makes it taste like candy. It makes kids *want* to brush their teeth, which makes it both a parent and kid buy," I say, remembering what Manny told me. "So naturally, it will fit right in here at Sweet Tooth."

Claudia nods. This is good. This is good.

"Every kid is going to want one," I continue. "And it's Manny's own invention! He's never invented before, so it's special. He's doing all the work himself, and then, of course, I'll take a look and see if what he's come up with is any good."

And that's when "nice" Claudia disappears, and "I wish I had never seen you" Claudia returns.

"What do you mean, 'see if it's any good'?" she asks, her expression even a little more stern than when I first arrived. "Haven't you tested it? Don't you already know if it's any good before you come into a store and waste someone's time?"

"Well, I—"

"I'm sorry, Mr. Sure, but I'm going to pass," she says standing up.

"Manny has no inventing track record. You have no sample to show me. So, I really can't justify my store placing an order for it, especially since it's unproven. You might as well be a whole new company. I'm sorry."

Claudia gestures to the door. Uh-oh. I guess I know what means . . .

I hop from my seat and walk out of the office, feeling pretty bad.

Kathy Jenkins, of course, is waiting there. "Billy, can I have a couple of words with—"

I walk right past her and out the front door.

Once I'm out on the street I realize that ignoring Kathy might not have been the smartest thing to do. I can only imagine what she'll write now—maybe that I'm a MEAN GUY?

But I'm really disappointed. And a little embarrassed. I'm really in no mood to speak to Kathy right now.

How could I have been so naive? I thought this sales thing was going to be easy. Especially once I saw how people react to the name Sure Things, Inc. As soon as I saw Claudia's expression change, I thought I had a guaranteed sale. But I guess that goes to show, nothing is guaranteed when it comes to selling. I sigh. I'm just going to have to work harder.

As I wander down the street, I search on my phone for directions to all the nearby stores.

Might as well try again!

I see that just a block away from here is a store called All Stuff Pharmacy. Sounds like a store that sells both toothbrushes *and* candy. Perfect!

A few minutes later I arrive. I comb my hair with my hands, straighten out my shirt, take a deep breath, and walk in.

You can do this! I tell myself.

This store is about four times bigger than Sweet Tooth. Aisle after aisle of stuff stretches out in front of me. I see toys, hair products, food, and even an aisle of pet goldfish! Hmm.

I step up to one of the eleven check-out counters.

"Excuse me, but I'd like to see the store manager," I say.

"Why? Is something wrong?" asks the teenager at the counter. "Are we out of something? Did you have trouble finding what you need? Did those kids switch the vitamins and the jelly beans again?"

"No, no," I say quickly. "I'm a salesperson with a new product."

The teenager raises an eyebrow, as if to ask, *You?*

"Okay," he says, then punches in a number on his intercom. "Someone would like to speak with you, sir," he says into it, and a man responds that he will be out shortly.

A few seconds later an older man with thick white hair approaches me.

"Hello, I'm Bert," the man says. "I'm the manager here at All Stuff Pharmacy. How can I help you?"

Thankfully, this time I know exactly how to begin.

"My name is Billy Sure. I represent Sure Things, Inc.," I say.

Bert smiles. "Sure Things, Inc.!" he repeats gleefully, and leads me through the door behind the counter, down a hall, and into his office. This time I take a seat in a soft, cushy chair. He sits down behind a big wooden desk.

"What have you got, Billy Sure of Sure Things, Inc.?" he asks.

I tell Bert all about the Candy Toothbrush.

"And think of all the additional toothpaste you'll sell once every kid with a Candy

Toothbrush wants to brush their teeth three, even four times a day!" I say.

Bert smiles and starts nodding more vigorously. He's going to place an order. I can just feel it. My first sale! I did it right this time. I did it! Here . . . it . . . comes. . . .

"Of course, all we have to do now is invent it!" I say, laughing.

I raise my hand to my mouth. Oh no. Did I just say that?!

Bert's whole expression instantly changes. His smile vanishes. His eyes narrow, and he leans over his desk toward me.

"The Candy Toothbrush hasn't been invented yet?" he asks, but doesn't wait for my response. "Look, I love this idea, I think it's going to be great, and my store will most likely place an order. But we can't order something unless we know it works."

He stands up and makes the now all-too-familiar gesture toward the door.

"Come back when you have a finished, working model," he says.

I can see that this meeting is over.

I walk out of the store, defeated again. This whole sales, marketing, business thing is way harder than I thought.

Will I EVER get the hang of it?

Chapter Five

Works in Progress

MY MIND RACES AS I WALK BACK TO THE OFFICE.

How come it's always so easy for Manny to start selling a new invention, but so hard for me? I don't think I can remember even one time that Manny came back from a sales run for a new invention dejected, failing to get at least some interest.

What if this whole switcheroo thing isn't such a great idea after all?

I arrive back at headquarters, take a deep breath, and walk in. As I come through the door, Philo lifts his head, narrows his eyes, and looks over at Manny, who is still sitting at my workbench. I can just see him thinking, *What is going on?*

Manny is hunched over, hard at work, moving parts around and sticking pieces together.

He is focused so intensely that it takes him a minute to realize that I'm back. Then he breaks out into a smile.

"Any luck?" Manny asks.

I shake my head. "Nah. You?"

"Take a look," he replies.

I see a toothbrush sitting on the workbench without any bristles on it. Instead, Manny has carved out tiny slivers of gummy candy and stuck each sliver into one of the little holes where the bristles usually go.

I don't know if this is going to work, but I'm impressed by Manny's method. He's a much more detailed, patient inventor than I am. I don't even want to think about having to place each one of those rubbery slivers into the tiny holes in the toothbrush.

"I'm not there yet," Manny says. "And I'm not positive this method will work. I am making progress. Slow progress, but I do feel like I am moving forward."

"Nice," I say.

"What happened at Sweet Tooth?" Manny asks.

I decide not to talk to him about my experience with Claudia.

"I ran into Kathy Jenkins," I say.

"Uh-oh," says Manny.

"Yeah, I know. I can't wait to read her article in tomorrow's *Right Next Door*," I say. "Should be a doozy."

Manny turns to the workbench. I appreciate him not pressing me on what went wrong with getting stores interested in the Candy Toothbrush.

If Manny is so dedicated to making this invention work, I think the least I can do is to change my approach when I try again. Two attempts down. Let's see if I have better luck next time.

"I think I'm going to head home, Manny," I say, needing to clear my head. "I'll try some new stores tomorrow."

Dinner that evening is pretty much a repeat performance of the last night. Emily sits, arms-crossed, lips tightly closed. She doesn't speak and she doesn't eat.

I don't know which is more SHOCKING.

After dinner I head up to my room for another round of *Sandbox XXL*. Not to brag or anything, but I'm on level twenty-two already.

Although I don't dream about *Sandbox XXL* when I finally put the game down and go to sleep, I certainly can't say that I have a peaceful night. I toss and turn in bed, imagining if I had to make sales calls with the monsters in *Sandbox XXL*. "Your teeth will be even more healthy!" I say. "ALL THE BETTER TO BITE AVATARS WITH!"

As soon as I wake up in the morning, I go to the *Right Next Door* website. Sure enough, the

lead story is an article by Kathy Jenkins. I read the headline:

SURE THINGS, INC.—BILLY SURE KID ENTREPRENEUR VS. MANNY REYES KID ENTREPRENEUR!

and I groan.

With a knot tightening in my stomach, I read the article:

Things are sure heating up at Sure Things, Inc., as reporter Kathy Jenkins found an EXCLUSIVE new story about the popular invention company. Sure Things, Inc.'s next invention—the Candy Toothbrush—will be on sale soon, but surprisingly, it is not a Sure Thing!

"For our next invention, I am going to be the company's CFO, and Manny is going to be our CEO and inventor," Billy Sure, of Sure Things, Inc. fame, said. "It's somewhat of a Sure Things, Inc. experiment. It's also a bit of a competition! But we all know I'm going to win!"

Although Billy Sure met with a few vendors for the Candy Toothbrush, no store buyers seemed interested.

"We love Sure Things, Inc. products," Claudia of the Sweet Tooth candy store said. "But unfortunately, we couldn't back this one up. It's just NOT a Sure Thing."

Other store owners felt the same way.

"Billy is an inexperienced CFO, and Manny is an inexperienced inventor," said Bert of All Stuff Pharmacy. "My store can't sell this."

Manny and Billy think this experiment is fun, but the big question is: Is Sure Things, Inc. DOOMED?!

Like the rest of the world, this reporter is waiting to find out!

I roll my eyes. *Of course.* She did it again.

This is just what I need—the whole world to know about my struggle as CFO or believing that Manny and I are competing against each other for real? That would never happen . . . would it? That is just not true.

Chapter Six

Soggy Cereal and Party Invites

I'M SO UPSET ABOUT THE ARTICLE, I ALMOST don't realize it's weird that Emily joins me at breakfast. But even silent Emily is hard to ignore. I look at her and wonder what she's been eating for the past few days. I haven't seen her open her mouth in a while. (I'm not complaining, but it's beginning to get weird.)

"Good morning," I say through a mouthful of cereal, though it comes out sounding more like "Mud Moomin."

"Mmph," Emily grunts, which is the most she's said to me in days.

She goes to the counter, grabs a bowl, and pours about three flakes of KRISPO-KRUNCHO FROSTED BITES, then fills the rest of the bowl with a *ton* of milk and joins me at the table.

Back at the table, Emily stares at the bowl, her chin resting in her hands. Her eyes dart back and forth between me and the cereal bowl. Again and again and again.

I'm not sure what she's expecting the flakes to do—put on a little show for her or turn all kinds of pretty colors—but she keeps on staring and not eating, and giving me a glare like she wants me to leave.

After a few minutes, when she realizes I'm not going anywhere, Emily pokes at the cereal, lifting a spoonful up close to her face and examining it. Then, without eating, she drops the cereal back into her bowl.

It's like she's waiting for her cereal to get really soggy before she eats it. But that is *super* weird. If there is one thing I know about Emily, it's that, like me, Emily *hates* soggy cereal. She always starts eating the second the milk hits the bowl. And she eats really fast so that even the last flake is still crunchy.

But for some reason, today she's waiting and waiting.

Again, she picks up a spoonful. This time she pokes at it with her finger, then returns it to the bowl and resumes her staring. I'm starting to think this is Emily's most absurd thing yet.

Normally I wouldn't resist giving Emily a hard time about this. But this morning I've got my own problems to deal with. Figuring out this whole switcheroo thing is hard enough, and now we have Kathy Jenkins to deal with again.

"Well, nice chatting with you, Em," I say, getting up and bringing my empty bowl to the sink. "Enjoy your GLOPPY MUSH."

"Mmm," Emily grunts again.

"Come on, Philo," I call out, heading for the front door. I glance back over my shoulder and see the back of Emily's head. She lifts the spoon up toward her face.

Well, at least she's eating, I think.

With Philo trotting happily along beside me, I bike over to the office, wondering as I ride what Manny thinks about Kathy's article. I'm trying my best to not let it upset me, but it's hard. It's tough enough doing this new CFO job without having to worry about people thinking bad things about us and the company.

Arriving at the office, I skid to a stop and scoot inside, followed by Philo, who takes his usual place in his doggy bed. Before I even get to say good morning, Manny turns to me from the workbench.

"Do you think REGULAR GREEN APPLE or SOUR GREEN APPLE would be more popular as our first Candy Toothbrush flavor?" he asks. Then, before I get a chance to respond: "I guess maybe it doesn't really matter since we can always expand the line by adding additional flavors later."

Manny is about to continue, but he catches himself, pauses, and looks right at me.

"Um, I'm sorry, Billy, I guess I slipped into my marketing hat for a second there. I know that's your job now. Just habit, I guess. What do *you* think?"

"Um, I guess either flavor would be fine to start with," I reply, not sure how I'm supposed to make a decision between green apple and *sour* green apple. "I mean, everyone likes apples, right? You kinda can't go wrong."

I try my best not to feel a little jealous of Manny. I know that he always has the best interest of the company in mind, but I wish that I could be as good a CFO as Manny appears to have become as an inventor.

Manny places a small sliver of green gummy onto his tongue. I stare as his face twists into various strange expressions. It's almost like he is trying to taste the flavor with his eyes, nose, and forehead, as well as his tongue.

A couple of minutes later he puts another small gummy sliver onto his tongue. This one is a lighter shade of green. And his face goes through the same scrunching movements.

"Definitely the *sour* green apple," he says, his face returning to normal.

I decide to change the subject.

"So, I guess you saw Kathy Jenkins's article in *Right Next Door*, huh?" I ask.

"Yeah, I saw it," Manny replies. "I laughed, shrugged it off, and put my mind back on the much more important topic at hand—regular apple versus sour apple."

"So, you're not worried?" I ask. "Kathy's articles always make me worry. The last time she wrote about us, kids avoided me in the hall at school. Not fun."

"I think this time even Kathy is stretching a bit too far," says Manny. "I think the best thing we can do is just ignore it. Pretend it's not there and it will go away, right?"

Following Manny's example, I push Kathy's article out of my mind and settle in at his desk to come up with an attack plan for today's sales pitches. After all, I need to learn from my mistakes and improve with each try.

I scan through a list of new stores that might be interested in the Candy Toothbrush. As I search, I practice my speech in my head:

Hello, wonderful store owner. I'm Billy Sure from Sure Things, Inc., and I'm here to give you a sneak peek at our brand-new invention. It's called the Candy Toothbrush and it's going to change the world. Okay, maybe not the world, but definitely the world inside your mouth!

Wait a minute. I don't even know what that means. Let me try again.

Hello, kind friend. I'm Billy Sure from Sure Things, Inc. and . . .

Well. The store owner isn't really my friend. I should stick with "store owner."

Hello, store owner. I'm Billy Sure from Sure Things, Inc., and I wanted you to be the first to know about our brand-new product.

But what if the owner of the next store I go to is friends with the owner of Sweet Tooth or the manager at All Stuff Pharmacy? What if they've already talked about my failed sales runs at those stores? Then they'd know that they are not the "first to know" and they'd catch me in a lie.

See?

This sales stuff is *not* easy, no matter how much wrapping paper I sold door to door in elementary school.

Manny must be able to tell I'm worried, because he looks over at me and smiles reassuringly. It's reason #360 that I'm glad he's my best friend and business partner. He just knows when I'm feeling down.

"Don't worry too much, Billy," he says. "It'll all work out. And at least we won't have to work on Saturday afternoon."

"Yeah," I say, and then it hits me. What's happening on Saturday afternoon? "Um, why aren't we working on Saturday?"

"It's Petula Brown's end-of-summer pool party," Manny says.

"That's weird," I say. "I never got an

invitation." Petula Brown is a girl in our class. I'm a little surprised that I wasn't invited to her pool party. After all, Petula came to my birthday party this year and we've always been friends.

"Oh," Manny begins. "Well, Petula only invited girls and said that the only way a boy can go is if a girl invites him. I assumed someone had already asked you."

What am I, Philo's dog food? Why didn't anyone ask me? I wonder. But I don't want to make Manny feel bad, so I try to be supportive.

"So who invited you?" I ask.

"Well, um, Petula kind of . . . *she* invited me," Manny says. "But don't worry, Billy," he adds quickly. "I'm sure someone will invite you, too. It's only Wednesday."

I mean, I'm happy that Manny will get to go to the party, but I also feel kinda bad. It's unfair! Why can't I just go to the party as Manny's friend? Or even as Petula's friend, since it's her party?

Why did Petula have to make this so

complicated by doing the whole "girl has to ask boy" thing? We're all friends. We all like to go to parties. Why mess it all up like this? Is this what life is going to be like now that we are eighth-graders?

I turn back to my lists and spreadsheets. I can't let this stupid party thing distract me. I don't have time to worry about that now—I have to stay focused and be the best salesperson I can be. *I'm going to sell the Candy Toothbrush,* I tell myself. I'm going to get it into every store and—

Oh, who am I kidding? I don't even know what my next move should be! I don't even know how to get invited to a pool party! Only Manny knows that.

Wait.

Manny?

What if I ask Manny to train me on how to be a good CFO? He *has* trained other people before, after all, like JADA PARIKH, the CFO of Definite Devices. And he must have taught her what to say, since the Funny Gummy was on sale at Sweet Tooth! So Jada must be great at selling, too.

And that's when it hits me. Manny is already busy working on inventing the Candy Toothbrush, but there's someone else I could ask for help.

Jada! Why don't I ask Jada to train me?!

Chapter Seven

Jada to the Rescue

I STARE AT MANNY'S COMPUTER SCREEN AND PICTURE myself being trained by Jada. That's when I realize: Of course I've *met* Jada, but I've never really talked to her. I usually just talk to Nat, the CEO of Definite Devices. She's always trying to sabotage me and Manny's partnership. She has a big crush on Manny and would love to have him work for her company. She was the one who pretended to be an Italian art collector to get the Sure family to move to Italy so Manny and I couldn't work together anymore! Jada seems nice, but what if she's just like Nat?

I guess I have nothing to lose by just asking her if she can help me. Still, I think I should tell Manny what my plan is. I don't want him to feel bad if I ask Jada to train me instead of him.

"So, I have an idea I want to run by you," I say to Manny.

"For a new invention?" Manny asks. "I thought that was my job now!"

We both laugh.

"No, actually I thought I could get some help about how to be a good CFO from Jada," I say. "I figure since you trained her, I'd be learning from the best—indirectly, anyway."

"Have you asked her?" Manny says.

"Not yet. I wanted to see what you thought."

"Sounds great to me," Manny says. Then he cracks a smile. "But I am *definitely* not asking NAT for inventor training."

Then Manny returns to fitting tiny gummy slivers into his prototype toothbrush.

I guess it's go time!

I scroll through my phone and click on Jada

Parikh. It rings . . . and rings . . . and rings . . .

"Hello?" says the voice on the other end.

"Hey, Jada, it's Billy—Billy Sure," I say. Oh man. That was dumb. She probably knew that already from caller ID. "Um, so I wanted to ask you a question."

"Nat didn't do something to hurt Sure Things, Inc. again?" Jada asks.

"No, no, not at all!" I answer quickly. I guess that makes sense—the last time Jada heard from me, it was when I busted Nat for almost making my whole family move across an entire ocean.

"Why I called is, Manny and I are trying a little experiment," I explain. "We're calling it a friendly switcheroo. For our next product, Manny is doing the inventing and I'm handling the marketing and sales."

"Interesting," she says flatly. "How's that going?"

"Well, Manny's working really hard on the invention, but I'm having a little trouble getting started on selling it. Which is actually why I'm calling. I was wondering . . . would you maybe be interested in helping me learn about being a good CFO? I think I need a teacher, and Manny is busy inventing, so I thought of you."

Jada is silent for a few seconds.

Uh-oh, she doesn't want to do it, and she's trying to figure out a nice way of telling me.

"I'd be happy to train you, Billy," she finally says. "It's the least I can do after all the trouble Nat has caused you in the past."

"Really?"

"Sure. Can you meet me later today?" Jada asks.

"Yeah! Um, where should we meet?"

"I'll meet you at the public library in an hour. How's that?"

"Great! I'll see you there!"

We say bye and hang up. It'll take me just under an hour to bike over to the library (it's a little far), so I start gathering my things.

"I'm heading over to the library to meet Jada," I tell Manny, who nods.

"Mmm . . . ," he replies, still completely

focused on his green gummy slivers.

As I head to the door, Philo stands up and stretches. He thinks it's time to go home.

"You stay here with Manny, boy," I say, pointing to Philo's bed. "I'll be back soon."

Poor Philo. That's the second time this week that I told him to stay here when I left. But what can I do? I know that I can't bring a dog into the library.

As I bike over to the library, my mind races. I dart between wondering why no one invited me to Petula's party, worrying about how awkward it might be training with Jada, and questioning if I can even sell the Candy Toothbrush at all.

Just as I'm thinking all of this, the library comes into view. I have to FOCUS! I need to learn as much as I can from Jada, so I push all these other thoughts away and chain my bike up to the rack outside.

Inside the library, I spot Jada sitting at a long table. I catch her eye and wave, then join her.

"Thanks so much for helping me," I say as I sit down.

"No problem," Jada says. "It'll be fun. And after all Manny taught me, I'm happy to share it with you. Let's get started."

Jada opens up her laptop. A blank spreadsheet appears on the screen.

"Spreadsheets are really helpful in keeping track of all the parts of your business," she explains. "These rows and columns can organize whatever you need—a list of all the places that might want to sell your invention, the ones that have agreed to sell it, then sales figures, store by store, once the invention comes out. I always keep notes in the last column, see? Like who I spoke to and what they said. If not I forget."

Hmm, that does make sense!

I scribble notes, trying to get down everything Jada says. As she talks, I realize that I feel like I can trust her. Unlike Nat, who is always trying to dupe us into something, Jada seems very sincere. I guess she's not responsible at all for Nat's little tricks.

Jada didn't have to go out of her way to help me today, I remind myself. I decide I'm going to tell her about the Candy Toothbrush. Her company already has the Funny Gummy—they aren't going to try to steal the idea, and besides, if Jada knows exactly what our next invention is, she might help me figure out how to sell it.

"So the invention that Manny is working on is called the Candy Toothbrush," I announce. I go on to give Jada the details, and basically rehash the sales pitch I've been giving time and time again.

"I think it's a cool idea," Jada says. "But why limit yourself to candy and convenience stores? I can see this in airports, novelty stores, even before the cash register at arts and craft stores as a gimmick . . ."

I wish I could write as fast as Jada thinks! She's got so many good ideas.

"As for a marketing plan," she continues, "I'd roll out with two or three flavors and two or three different colors. That way, you could introduce new colors and flavors each year to keep the product fresh and keep customers coming back. You know, you really should do something like that for your older products, too," she says.

"Wow!" I say, writing so fast my pen is a BLUE BLUR. "Actually, Manny mentioned something similar for the All Ball and the

Sibling Silencer. This is fantastic, Jada."

"You can keep track of all this on a spreadsheet like the one I showed you," she says.

Jada must have noticed how fast I was writing because she pauses for a moment to let me catch up.

Then she continues.

"Something else that will help you is a SELL SHEET," Jada explains. "It's one page with colorful graphics that lists all the great things about your invention, to make it easier for busy buyers to quickly see why your invention is such a good idea. And you leave it with them whenever you go somewhere, so they can think about the product when you're not around."

I immediately start making a list of all the good features of the Candy Toothbrush. And I can already picture some cool graphics to make the sell sheet more interesting.

A short while later Jada's cell phone beeps.

"That's my mom," she says, closing her laptop. "I have to get home for dinner."

"Thank you so much, Jada," I say as we leave the library. "You're really great."

Jada turns and smiles at me. Is she blushing? "Thanks, Billy," she says, and she hops on her bike.

Then she notices my backpack—which has a giant *Sandbox XXL* keychain on it. "Do you play?" she asks.

"Yeah! I got to level twenty-three this morning," I say proudly.

Jada smiles.

"Cute," she says.

"Do you play?" I ask.

"Yeah, I play," Jada says, and takes her phone out of her pocket. She opens up the *Sandbox XXL* app.

WHAT?!

DOUBLE WHAT?!

Hold up.

No.

WAY.

I gasp! Jada doesn't just *play*. I look at her ranking. She is the NUMBER THREE player in the world!

My jaw drops. But before I can say anything else, Jada smirks and says, "See you, Billy." Then she peddles away.

Forget this CFO thing. I think I need to ask Jada to give me pointers on *Sandbox XXL!*

I think about how awesome Jada is as I peddle back to the office. She's kind of quiet, but super funny in her own way. I'm glad she took the time to help me, but I'm also glad I got the chance to get to know her a little better. Also, I kind of feel like I was just in the presence of a gaming celebrity, which I guess she kind of is.

I stop by the office, grab Philo, and arrive home in time for dinner, where I discover that Dad has made hamburgers. That's it . . . just plain hamburgers. My dad is, um, let's say an "interesting" chef. He usually doesn't cook just plain burgers. You're more likely to come home to prune-radish-cheesecake burgers. I guess you've got to hand it to him for creativity! It looks like tonight's dinner is going to be yummy!

Of course, that being said, it *is* still Dad's dinner, so a bunch of weird toppings are spread across the table—toppings like mango, guava, whipped cream, and cans of tuna—at least, I *think* it's tuna. It could very well be cat food. But, fortunately, all these are optional.

As I sit at the table, I notice Emily grab a burger and get up from the table. To my absolute *horror*, she plops the entire thing—bun and all—into a blender!

Yes, a blender! A hamburger smoothie sounds like something my dad would dream up! What crazy world is this?!

Mmmm! Burger!

WHIRP! WHIRP! WHIRP! She turns the blender on and it becomes instant mush. Not unlike her soggy cereal, I should say.

I stare at the blender in disbelief as a gross slop of gray and brown mush spins around and around.

"Um, Em, what are you doing?" I ask. I feel queasy, and it's hard to get the words out without gagging.

Emily unsurprisingly shoots a nasty glare in my direction.

Is she finally going to say something? Is her no-talking thing over?

Not yet. She just stares at me and scrunches up her face.

She shakes her head. I shake mine back.

Well, this isn't going anywhere. I'm just going to come right out and ask her.

"Emily, why won't you talk?" I ask.

She says nothing.

"Emily, you gotta talk," I say again. "Or I'm going to talk and talk and talk and talk—"

"You want me to talk?!" Emily barks. "Look at this!" She screams, making me realize that this is the first time in days I've heard her voice. I'm instantly sorry I asked.

And I notice, now that she has opened her mouth, that she is wearing *braces* on her teeth!

Huh. Now it all makes sense! She didn't want me to see them, and they probably make chewing hard!

"Is that what this is all about?" I ask. "Braces?"

"They are sooooo embarrassing," Emily says. She puts her hand in front of her mouth so I can't see her teeth.

"I don't think so," I tell her. "Lots of people have to wear braces. Allison Arnolds has them. She changes the colors on hers every few weeks. I think they're kind of cool."

What I don't tell Emily is the only reason I ever noticed Allison's braces is that I used to have a teeny tiny crush on her, and sometimes seeing her new braces color was the best part of my day.

"You try wearing braces, then!" Emily snaps back. She pours the liquefied burger into a glass, then sticks a straw in.

Between being yelled at and the slurping sound Emily starts to make, I slink away from the table. I think I've officially lost my appetite.

Chapter Eight

Party Problems

THE NEXT DAY AT THE OFFICE I FIND MANNY STILL placing slivers of gummy into the toothbrush. I fill him in on my meeting with Jada, but leave out the part about her being a *Sandbox XXL* celebrity. The way she showed me—it was like she wanted to keep it quiet among friends. It felt kinda cool to be let in on her secret. Especially such an awesome one!

"Sounds like she gave you some great business tips," Manny says.

"Well, she learned from the best," I say, smiling.

Sitting at Manny's computer, I set up a new spreadsheet, just like the one that Jada showed me. I fill it in with the stores I've already visited, a few places I'm planning on visiting next, and a list of all the great things about the Candy Toothbrush.

Then I take this info and start working on a sell sheet.

When that's finished, I decide to reach out to CANDY MART, the biggest candy chain in the country. Why not go for the best? After all, I believe in this invention. Truly. Now that I have some confidence, I decide to call the buyer at Candy Mart.

"Hi, this is Billy Sure, president of Sure Things, Inc., and I'd like to set up an appointment with your national buyer to give you a sneak peek at our latest invention," I say. ("President," Jada told me, is a good title to give out.)

"Hold, please."

Uh-oh. I've heard *that* before. Is this going to be another case of putting me on hold forever?

I can feel the burst of confidence I just had draining. How long should I stay—

"This is DORIS BEAN, head buyer for Candy Mart," a voice on the other end of the phone says suddenly. "Is this Billy Sure?"

"Yes, thanks for talking . . . I mean, thanks for the opportunity to share our—"

"Do you have information that you can e-mail me?" Ms. Bean asks.

"Um, of course," I reply. "I can send it right along."

"Good. I'll put my secretary on the line. He'll give you my e-mail address."

"Great! Thank you for—"

Click.

I guess that's it.

A few seconds later her secretary comes on and gives me Ms. Bean's e-mail address. I quickly e-mail her a copy of the sell sheet, hoping that I did exactly what I was supposed to do.

Then I go back into the spreadsheet, updating it with notes from my talk with Doris.

"Has anyone asked you to Petula's party yet?" Manny asks, interrupting my thoughts.

The party! Ugh. Just what I need to think about now!

"No, not yet," I say.

But you know what? That party with all its rules about who can invite who is dumb. I feel that way about middle school formals, too. You can have just as much fun with friends as with a date.

But even though I think that, I still want to go to the party. I decide to text Allison Arnolds. If she's going to the party, and if the conversation goes well, maybe she'll think of asking me.

I have barely typed the first few letters of my text to Allison when **BEEP!** I get an e-mail, this time from Doris Bean!

This looks interesting. Can you meet with me tomorrow morning? Say, 9:30? —DB

"Wow!" I shout.

"Did someone just ask you to the party?" Manny asks.

"'DORIS!'" I shout.

"Doris?" Manny laughs. "Is she going into eighth grade? I don't know her."

I laugh. "No, Doris Bean—she's the national buyer for Candy Mart. She wants to meet with me about the Candy Toothbrush!"

"Nice, Billy!" Manny says. "Congrats!"

This is fantastic. All I did was use what Jada taught me. Only now I've got to prepare for my meeting tomorrow—and text Allison Arnolds, of course.

I'm about to go back to writing to Allison when I notice that Philo is up and pacing.

"Looks like Philo needs to go out," I say. "Be back in a bit. Come on, boy."

Philo follows me out the front door.

It actually feels good to be outside and walking. As Philo and I stroll though the neighborhood, I spot someone familiar up ahead.

When I'm close enough, I see that it's Peter

MacHale, a kid who goes to my school. Peter is like a one-man newsfeed. Whenever anything happens, he always has to be the first to tell me.

Today Peter is mowing Manny's neighbor's lawn. It's probably his summer job. I suddenly am really happy my job is inventing—I'd be a *terrible* lawn mower! I'd probably get distracted and mow strange shapes into people's lawns.

Peter spots me and turns off his mower.

"Hey, Billy!" he shouts, waving.

"Hi, Peter," I say. Philo kicks at some grass.

"Billy, did you hear? Petula Brown is having a pool party this Saturday!"

"I heard, yeah," I reply.

"Are you going?" he asks.

"I hope so. I just haven't . . . um . . . been officially invited yet," I say, reminding myself to text Allison as soon as I get back to the office. "Are you? Did anyone invite you?

"I am! And yes," Peter announces proudly. "I was so happy! Allison Arnolds asked me to go. We were lab partners last year. I thought she hated me, but I guess not."

My stomach drops like I just swallowed a bowling ball.

"That's awesome, Peter," I croak out.

"Well, TIME IS MONEY," Peter says, starting up his mower again. "See ya Saturday, Billy! I'm *sure* someone will ask you!" Then he laughs. It's not the first time he's made a "sure" joke before, and I doubt it'll be his last.

I wave good-bye and head back to the office.

I can't believe Allison asked Peter MacHale! But I do have to say, I'm glad that I didn't text her yet. That could have been really embarrassing.

I know Peter and Manny think someone will ask me to the pool party, but it sounds like everyone has asked someone already. Unless . . .

Samantha Jenkins! Samantha Jenkins might ask me. Despite the articles her mother writes, Samantha has always been my biggest fan. She did want to talk to me at Sweet Tooth, didn't she?

I arrive back at the office energized by my walk, and feeling pretty good about the possibility that I might actually be going to this party.

I grab my phone and give Samantha a call.

"Hi, Billy!" Samantha says excitedly when she picks up. "How are you?"

I decide to cut to the chase.

"Hey, Samantha. Have you heard about PETULA BROWN'S POOL PARTY this Saturday?" I ask, trying my best to sound like I'm just making idle conversation.

"Oh yes, Billy!" she says, "I'm really looking forward to going! Will I be seeing you there?"

"You know that a boy can only go if a girl asks him," I say carefully.

"Oh, I know," Samantha says. "That's why I asked Clayton!"

My eyes widen. Clayton?!

Samantha, my "biggest fan," asked Clayton Harris to the pool party?! Don't get me wrong, I like Clayton a lot. And I'm thrilled at how he really found himself through the Inventors Club. And he even helps out Sure Things, Inc. with new inventions from time to time.

But, sheesh! Clayton wouldn't even *know* Samantha if it wasn't for me! Okay, Billy, stop feeling so sorry for yourself.

"That's great, Samantha," I finally say.

"Yeah, I'll see you at the party, Billy! Talk to you later!" She hangs up.

I guess, like Peter, Samantha just figures that someone must have asked me. Some inventor celebrity, huh? Or . . . CFO celebrity, I should say!

I gather my materials for tomorrow's meeting with Doris at Candy Mart and try to focus on that. When I've done all I can, I figure it'd be best just to head home.

"I'm gonna go, Manny," I say. "I want to get a good night's sleep before my big meeting tomorrow."

"I'll be here, perfecting the prototype," Manny says. "Good luck, though I don't think you'll need it!"

I hope I don't, I think as Philo and I head outside.

• • •

I arrive at home to find Emily standing at the kitchen counter. She has two bowls in front of her, one filled with yogurt, the other with mashed potatoes. She puts a tiny bit of yogurt onto a spoon and gently slips it past her braces. Then she does the same thing with the mashed potatoes.

I actually feel sorry for Em. She's really struggling with the whole braces thing.

I head to my room and shoot off a text to Jada. In all my excitement I forget to tell her about my big appointment tomorrow. I've got to thank her! Because, of course, I wouldn't even have gotten the appointment without her help.

A few seconds later I get a text back from her:

Can I come with you for moral support?

Wow! She wants to come along. How cool is that? I text her back and we set up a time to meet the next morning.

At dinner that night it appears the Sure family's delicious takeout/normal-hamburger streak is over.

"Tonight's dinner is MEXICAN, ITALIAN, CHINESE DELIGHT!" Dad announces happily as he slaps large blobs onto each of our plates.

"What exactly is Mexican, Italian, Chinese delight?" I ask, watching Emily scowl at the dish. I'm glad that she was able to eat her soft snack earlier, and I honestly kind of regret not doing the same.

"Isn't it obvious?" Dad replies. "It's a beef taco stuffed inside a pasta shell stuffed inside a dumpling. Nice, right?"

"Very creative, Bryan," Mom says.

I laugh, knowing full well that Mom is just being kind. She would much rather order in real Mexican, Italian, or Chinese food any day.

I take a bite. It's actually not that bad. When you break it all down, it's just pasta, crunchy taco, and meat. In fact, I don't even use any GROSS-TO-GOOD POWDER on it.

"What is that flavor in the middle of all this, Dad?" I ask, helping myself to another one.

"Curry," Dad replies proudly. "I realized that I left out Indian food, so I added lots of curry to the whole dish."

No one reminds him that he forgot to call this Mexican, Italian, Chinese, Indian delight. Also, I wonder if this dinner can help bring peace to the world.

After dinner I head to my room. I don't even play that much *Sandbox XXL*. (Although I still play a little. I'm on level thirty now after some pointers from Jada.) I need rest. After all, tomorrow is a big day!

Chapter Nine

Meetings and Mouths

I WAKE UP EARLY THE NEXT MORNING FOR MY meeting with Doris Bean. If this goes well, it will pretty much guarantee that the Candy Toothbrush will be a hit. Or that I can do this whole CFO thing, anyway!

I put on my nicest shirt and dress pants. I even take the bus downtown, so I don't risk getting dirty riding my bike. Jada is already there when I arrive, waiting outside the Candy Mart headquarters.

Jada looks very nice. She's dressed up in a suit. I almost don't recognize the girl with beat-up jeans who so casually revealed that she's a world-famous *Sandbox XXL* player.

"Here we go," Jada says as we walk into the building.

If you thought the whole interior design at Sweet Tooth was impressive, the lobby of the Candy Mart HQ is UNBELIEVABLE! The

chairs are shaped like giant candy canes. If you sit on one, it kinda looks like you are hanging in midair from a red and white striped hook!

The carpet has images of all the famous products that Candy Mart sells, from gummies to candy bars to lollipops and on and on. They look so delicious that I almost want to start eating the carpet, but then I have to tell myself that the carpet won't taste nearly as delicious as it looks.

Jada and I step up to the front desk, which is shaped like a huge, round peanut butter cup.

"May I help you two?" asks the woman behind the peanut butter cup.

"Hi there. We are Billy Sure and Jada Parikh, here to see Doris Bean," I say.

The woman types something into her computer and smiles curtly.

"Down the hall and to your left," the woman mumbles.

"You ready?" Jada asks as we walk toward the big door.

"As ready as I'll ever be," I say.

"You'll do fine, Billy! Just be yourself. Doris Bean is no level-eighteen *Sandbox XXL* martian-shark." She smiles.

I laugh. That is true. And if I could beat that martian-shark with its radioactive teeth, then I can definitely beat this!

We reach Doris Bean's office and I knock on the door.

"Please come in," says a voice on the other side.

I open the door. The office is HUGE. To my surprise, there isn't any candy anywhere. There's just a normal-looking desk, and a normal-looking meeting table, and a bunch of normal-looking chairs. With all the candy images out in the lobby, I'm totally craving a sweet right now, but I guess I'll just have to get to business at hand.

"Billy, it is so nice to meet you," says the woman inside. "I'm Doris Bean. And Jada! It is so nice to see you again. We are so pleased with the success of the Funny Gummy."

"Thank you," Jada says politely. "Actually, the success of that product made me want to come with Billy. I really believe in this one, Ms. Bean."

Huh! I wonder if that's why Jada wanted to come with me! *Of course* she'd know Doris. Definite Devices's Funny Gummy is Candy Mart's biggest seller right now.

Ms. Bean holds up a printed copy of the sell sheet I e-mailed her. "So tell me about the Candy Toothbrush," she says.

Here you go, Billy. Just do it!

I begin:

"As you see from the sell sheet, the Candy Toothbrush is being produced by the same company as other successful products like the SIBLING SILENCER, the ALL BALL, and the MAGICAL MICROPHONE. And while Sure Things, Inc.'s products are always *fun*, this time, our invention is even *sweeter*—we're bringing the same innovative technology that our company is known for to a product that will help encourage even the fussiest kids to brush their teeth."

Wow! Listen to me. I sound legit!

I continue: "We already have a ton of interest out there, but we are offering a SPECIAL DISCOUNT to the first store that comes on board—which could very well be Candy Mart, if you act fast."

"Very interesting, Billy," says Ms. Bean, leaning back in her seat. "I like your confidence, and the track record of Sure Things, Inc."

She takes out her glasses and spends some time going over the sell sheet. She grabs a calculator and punches a few numbers in.

Then she turns to us.

"Based on my projections, I'm going to go with my gut here," she starts. My hands feel clammy. Oh no. She is going to pass. What if she passes on the product? What will I do then?!

I start panicking, and that's when my legs start twitching—

"Count Candy Mart in as the first store to sign on for the Candy Toothbrush!" Doris says, clapping.

Candy Mart is *in*? Did I just hear that right?! Stay calm, Billy. STAY CALM!!!

But I can't help it. I break out into a *huge* smile and high-five Jada! I go to high-five Doris, but instead she stands up and extends her hand.

"Keep me posted about when this invention will be going into full-scale production," she says as I reach out and shake her hand. "My legal department will be in touch to draw up the contracts. Thanks for coming in. It was very nice to meet you, Billy—and of course, to see you again, Jada."

"Thank you," Jada and I say in unison. Then we turn and leave before I wake up from what must be a dream.

Outside, Jada is absolutely giddy.

"I am *so proud of you!*" she squeals. "You were amazing, Billy! Absolutely amazing."

Jada hugs me and we both jump up and down together.

"I couldn't have done it without your help," I say. "Thanks, Jada."

"Just you wait until you get to level thirty-one of *Sandbox XXL*," Jada says. "Then you'll really be asking for my help. The monster in that level is *really* hard. "

I laugh, and we part ways. I take the bus back to the office feeling pretty good. As I walk in, Manny turns around. He's got a humongous smile on his face.

Level 32 Monster

"I have great news!" we both say at the same time. Then we both laugh.

"YOU GO FIRST," I say.

"I'm ready for the test run of my Candy Toothbrush prototype," Manny announces.

"That's perfect, because I just sold the Candy Toothbrush to Candy Mart!" I say proudly.

"Way to go, Billy!" Manny says, coming over to me to share a high five.

"So, let's get testing, shall we?"

"First, I should get my teeth nice and messy," Manny says. He looks around the room. "I know! I'll eat a supermessy slice of pizza from our pizza-dispensing machine."

When Manny and I set up World Headquarters, the first thing we did was install some fancy perks. One of those perks was a pizza-dispensing machine. Another of those perks is a foosball table.

The pizza machine is by far my favorite thing, ever. All you do is enter the toppings you want, press a button, and a perfectly-cooked slice of hot pizza comes sliding out! If only I could get one of those for my house . . . Maybe we could even program it to make soggy slices for Emily!

"Let's see," Manny says, staring at the choices listed on the front of the machine. "I have to make my teeth messy and my breath smelly. . . . How about EXTRA CRUNCHY, EXTRA SAUCE, EXTRA GARLIC, and EXTRA ONION?"

"Might as well add some EXTRA ANCHO-VIES too!" I say.

Manny nods and presses the buttons. BEEP! A steaming, gooey slice of *really* stinky pizza with tons of toppings comes sliding out.

Manny takes a few bites, then smiles broadly at me, revealing his gunky teeth, covered with bits of onion and sauce.

Hey, maybe I should have worked on the Candy Toothbrush a long time ago. This trial-and-error part looks like fun.

"Okay, now for the first test of the Candy Toothbrush," Manny says between bites.

He walks over to the sink and pulls out the prototype. It looks just like a regular toothbrush, but I know how incredibly detailed it is. He puts regular old toothpaste on the bristles and starts brushing. I notice a lot of fun-looking bubbles come from the brush!

"It's working!" he says through a foamy mouth. "Sour apple! Man, is it *sour*!"

A few seconds later Manny rinses his mouth out with water. He breathes into his hand and smells it.

"Tasted like sour apple, but my breath is minty fresh!" he says as I look at my spreadsheet. "Billy, I think the Candy Toothbrush is going to be a BIG SUCCESS!"

"Yay us!" I cheer. I'm thrilled for Manny, but to be honest, I kinda feel a little jealous. I mean, the *first* prototype of the *very first* invention he ever built works *perfectly*, the first time he tries it. I'd never tell him this, of course, but I wish I could do that when we switch back!

If we ever switch back, I think now. Oh no. What if Manny decides he wants to invent full-time?

I can't let that get to me. I have to be positive.

Yeah, but you did make your first sale, I remind myself. Then I smile. *I* had a pretty great day too! But I can't rely on just one store—even if it is a place as great as Candy Mart—to carry the invention. So I get back to work, building my list of stores to contact.

"I think Philo is still a bit confused by us working at each other's desks," I tell Manny as I look across at Philo, who has his paws draped off the doggy bed.

"Mmm," Manny mumbles.

"Hey, did you catch the Hyenas game the other day?" I ask. It may seem like we don't talk a lot at the office, but Manny and I are best friends, and we talk about *everything*. "Carl Bourette hit *three* homeruns!"

"Mhm," Manny mutters.

"Oh, and I'm not really that upset anymore about Petula's pool party," I say. "It would have been nice to go, but I just need to accept no one is inviting me. But you must be excited about going. Petula is really nice."

"Mhm," Manny grunts again.

What's going on with Manny? All he's doing is grunting and mumbling. Oh no. Has he joined Emily in the "I'm not talking anymore" club? Did he get braces in the past hour?

I decide I have *got* to make Manny talk! And since Manny is a scaredy cat, I know exactly the way to do it!

When Manny isn't looking, I grab an old sheet and throw it over Philo. Philo, who wants to shake it off but isn't exactly coordinated, starts walking toward Manny like a short, dog-shaped ghost.

I also happen to know that Manny is really afraid of ghosts.

"YAAAA!" I yell, pointing at Philo. "What is that thing? Is that a GHOST?"

Manny turns around and sees Ghost Philo scuffling across the floor. He leaps out of his chair and yells, "AAAAAAH!"

Aha!

That's when I see what Manny was mumbling about—his teeth are green! Not the kind of light green like candy sometimes makes teeth. No, these are full-on green, like a lawn in spring!

Chapter Ten

Switching the Switcheroo

MANNY SHUTS HIS MOUTH QUICKLY, BUT IT'S TOO late. I've seen it all.

"I think I just discovered a side effect of the Candy Toothbrush," Manny admits.

Okay, so I feel really bad that Manny's teeth are green, but I can't help but feel a teeny-tiny bit better about my own inventing abilities, knowing that Manny has run into the same problems with early prototypes as I do.

"How long is this going to last?" Manny groans. "I can't go to Petula's party tomorrow with green teeth!"

I find myself giggling, even though I do feel bad for Manny. Then I get an idea.

I hurry to my workbench and quickly tweak the formula for the INVISIBILITY SPRAY, reworking it so that it is both safe to eat and will make teeth normal color again by making the green invisible until it wears off.

Manny rubs some on his teeth. A few seconds later they are back to normal.

"Thanks, Billy," he says. "I guess it's back to the drawing board for me!"

On my way home I think about how quickly I was able to retool the Invisibility Spray formula to help Manny. It makes me happy to think that my inventing skills are still pretty sharp, even if I haven't been inventing much lately.

That evening after my shower I notice the bathroom counter is covered with all kinds of weird tooth and braces stuff—Emily's equipment, I guess. I see special floss, tiny rubber bands, and some goopy stuff in a container that is labeled "mouth wax." The entire counter is filled with this stuff. How many products do you *need* for braces?!

Then I feel kinda bad. I didn't realize Emily had to change her entire toothbrush routine. If only the Candy Toothbrush . . .

I pause. The lightbulb in my head goes off.

Lots of kids have braces. What if we made the Candy Toothbrush easy to use for kids with braces? Like, make it so you wouldn't need special picks for the brackets? I bet it would be an even bigger seller! We could make it have a switch with options—one for kids with braces and one for kids without.

I'll have to talk with Manny about this tomorrow and see what he thinks.

· · ·

When I wake up the next morning, I'm surprisingly sleepy. I thought I'd rested a lot. . . . What happened? As I walk past my desk I see something stretched out across the top. Leaning in for a closer look, I see that it's blueprints.

I must have invented in my sleep, like I usually do when I'm working on a new product for Sure Things, Inc. But I'm not working on a new product. So what did I sleep invent?

I scan the blueprints and discover that I have sleep-invented plans for the perfect Candy Toothbrush!

Looking at the blueprints more closely, I see that I have come up with a design for a

Candy Toothbrush that works for kids with or without braces. And it works better than a regular toothbrush—getting all those hard-to-reach places!

Not only that, but I can see where Manny went wrong and why his teeth turned green. My blueprints bypass that problem completely.

This is perfect! This is fantastic! I should text Manny right away!

Or should I?

Normally, I would want to him to know about sleep-invented blueprints as soon as possible. But this invention is his, not mine. I don't want to step on Manny's toes. He's been so careful about not interfering with my marketing and sales plans. I'm not sure what to do.

I roll up the blueprints, slip them into my backpack, and head out to the office. I'm not entirely sure what I'm going to tell Manny. Maybe I should wait it out, and tell him only if he asks for help?

I arrive at World Headquarters to find

Manny hard at work on tweaking his Candy Toothbrush prototype. I sit at his desk and start entering numbers into a spreadsheet, following my whole "wait it out" plan.

I feel like I'm on the edge of my seat!

Every few seconds I glance over to Manny and stare longingly at my workbench. That's where I want to be. That's where I *should* be. Especially now that I have the solution to all the problems with this invention. I wish I was sitting there, tinkering and tweaking the Candy Toothbrush, based on *my* blueprints!

I go back to my spreadsheet, typing in notes about the e-mails I've exchanged with the buyers at Taco! Taco! Taco! (they think the Candy Toothbrush might be a great addition to their kids meals—I ate at Taco! Taco! Taco! once, and I can guarantee that it's a good idea). A few minutes later I look up and see Manny staring at me . . . or rather, at his own desk.

"So you've only sold the Candy Toothbrush to one place at this time, right, partner?" Manny asks, COOL AS A CUCUMBER.

"Yup, but it *is* Candy Mart," I point out. "But, yeah, I haven't gotten any more bites. Potentially Taco! Taco! Taco!, and I'm meeting later with a dentist to see if he wants to stock the Candy Toothbrush in his office. Jada's coming with me."

Manny scratches his head and stares at me. An uncomfortable look comes across his face, like he's got some bad news he doesn't want to tell me.

Uh-oh. My hands feel sweaty. Manny *never* looks this stressed. Is something wrong? Does he know I sleep-invented? Is he mad at me?

Manny finally speaks.

"So, after yesterday's . . . er, *incident* . . . with the Candy Toothbrush, I actually tried to sleep-invent," he admits.

Wow! Manny sleep-inventing. Who knows, maybe I'm not the only one who can do it?

"How'd it go?" I ask.

"Not so great," Manny says. "I'm not really good at it like you are, Billy. Here, I'll show you."

Manny opens up his briefcase and pulls out a rolled-up blueprint. I walk over to the workbench just as he unrolls it.

It's on blueprint paper, but it doesn't look like a blueprint. It's just a bunch of squiggles!

I look at the paper a little more carefully. Hmm, *is* it just a bunch of squiggles? There is something vaguely familiar about it. I tilt my head from one side to the other. Then I reach down and turn the paper on its side.

BINGO!

There it is! I see it!

"Manny, this isn't an invention blueprint," I say. "It's not a bunch of squiggles, either." I pause, waiting for this to sink in.

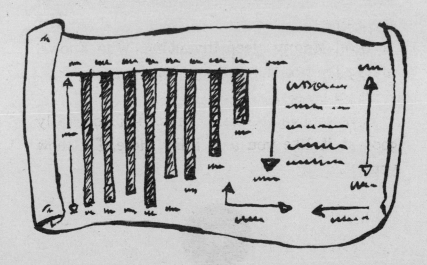

"It's a MARKETING PLAN for the Candy Toothbrush! Look at these lines. It's a graph, with projected sales numbers, a geographic marketing strategy . . . do you realize what you've done?"

Manny stares at the plan and scratches his head.

"You've sleep-invented a marketing plan!" I say. "Your *real* talent came out when you slept, just like mine does."

I think the time is right to show Manny what I came up with last night. I pull the blueprints out of my backpack and roll them out on top of Manny's.

"I wasn't going to show you these . . . at least not right away, because I didn't want you to feel bad," I explain. "But I accidentally sleep-invented last night too."

Manny looks at my plan and smiles.

"This is perfect," he says. "It not only solves the green teeth problem, but it looks like you have a special setting that will work for people with braces!"

"Yup, that's all part of it."

"It's fantastic. What made you think about kids with braces?"

"Long story," I say. "I'll fill you in later."

"So it looks like we both had the same idea," Manny says. "Subconsciously, anyway. We each did the thing that we're best at."

"I had no idea that SLEEP-MARKETING was even possible," I say.

"Me neither," says Manny, laughing. "And *I'm* the guy who did it!"

Manny looks over my blueprints as I review his marketing plan.

"Do you think maybe this SWITCHEROO we've been doing isn't as good an idea as we first thought?" he asks. "I mean, I hate admitting defeat as much as you do, but maybe we're just not cut out for the switch. Do you think it's time to go back to each doing what we are good at?"

I want to cheer. This is exactly what I've been thinking! I'm glad Manny was the one to suggest it, though.

"Yes!" I say, almost too excitedly.

"Then I think we can say that the time for our Sure Things switcheroo is officially over!" says Manny, clapping his hands.

A great feeling of relief washes over me. And I think about how this is reason #990 why Manny is my best friend and CFO. He's honest, he knows what he can and can't do, and he knows how to end things gracefully.

All right, so maybe those are reasons #990, #991, and #992, but you know what I mean.

I quickly text Jada to let her know that Manny is taking over the marketing side of the Candy Toothbrush, so that there is no need for us to meet up at the dentist's office.

For the first time since Manny and I switched back to our talents, I feel kinda down. I'm not sure, but I think I'm disappointed that I'm not going to see Jada this afternoon.

Manny and I switch seats. As soon as I sit down and spread a bunch of parts out next to my blueprints, that MAGICAL FEELING I always get when I'm inventing returns!

"Farmer Billy"

The best part of the switcheroo—in addition to really understanding how hard Manny's job is—is that it showed me that I was really meant to be an inventor. I've had my moments where I wonder. When my prototype for the BEST TEST told me I should be a spinach farmer instead of an inventor, I wondered if I was making the right choices. And it's often hard juggling the pressure of being in middle school and being a world-famous inventor and CEO. Sometimes I just want to relax. But even when I'm not trying to think about inventing, I inevitably . . . INVENT!

After an hour of intensive work on the prototype, I feel like it's in pretty good shape for testing. But before I get the chance, I hear Manny squeal with delight.

"Guess what?" he says, hanging up his phone. "I just got that dentist's office on board!"

"Without even going there?"

"Yup. Looks like my sleep-marketing plan is ready to roll. Or should I say, *unroll*!"

Manny unrolls his blueprint paper and turns to his computer.

"Look at this," he says.

I scoot across the room and lean over to see the screen. Manny has the *Right Next Door* website open to the article Kathy Jenkins wrote about us a few days ago. I had actually forgotten all about it. I wonder why Manny is bringing it up now that we are both in such a good mood.

"Check out the comments under the article, Billy," Manny says.

I groan. If I've learned anything since becoming a minor celebrity, it's that you *never* read online comments. *Ever. Never ever.*

What does *Right Next Door* have against Sure Things, Inc.? They make good stuff. My son plays with the All Ball every day.

I happen to know Billy Sure and Manny Reyes, and they are nothing like these articles make them out to be.

Comment after comment reads like these.

"I'm guessing we won't be having any more trouble from Kathy Jenkins, huh?" I say, realizing just what this might mean. NO MORE MEAN THINGS in the news!

"So," says Manny, obviously feeling giddy. "Are we ready to test your new sleep-invented prototype?"

"Yup," I say. "And since you were *so brave* last time, I'll volunteer to eat the pizza this time around."

I go over to our pizza-dispensing machine and make a slice with garlic, garlic, and more garlic, orange gummy bears, and black olives.

Out comes the steaming slice. Looking it over, I wish I had some Gross-to-Good Powder handy, but I gobble it down anyway, being sure to rub the toppings all over my teeth.

When I'm done, I smile and show my teeth to Manny.

"Yuck," he says. "Your teeth look like some kind of strange rainbow of gross colors all running together."

"Perfect!" I say. Then I take the new prototype, set it for "no braces," and brush my teeth. The sour apple flavor immediately blocks out all the weird flavors I put on my pizza. It really makes the mint toothpaste taste like delicious, tasty, sour apple candy!

Okay, here's the moment of truth. I look in the mirror. My teeth are gleaming white! Not green! They look even nicer than they did before!

"It works, Manny!" I say. "Look!"

I smile at Manny. He smiles right back and gives me a thumbs-up.

We celebrate then with normal cheese pizza

(Manny gets triple sauce, per usual). It really does feel like a celebration—I think we're both just happy to be back in our own roles. I make a few more prototypes for testing and put them in my backpack.

"Billy, I still feel really bad that you're not going to PETULA'S PARTY TOMORROW," Manny says. "So I was thinking. What if I don't go? I really wish you could come, but since you can't, I don't mind staying here and hanging out with you."

In all the excitement about switching our roles back and the successful prototype test, I actually forgot all about the party.

"Nah," I say. "It's no big deal. You go. I'll have fun playing *Sandbox XXL* at home. No worries."

I turn to Philo.

"Come on, boy. Let's go home," I say.

Chapter Eleven

Party Time!

ON THE WAY HOME I FEEL SURPRISINGLY OKAY ABOUT not going to Petula's party. Sure, it would be fun, and I know most of the kids who'll be there, but with the success of the Candy Toothbrush prototype and with Manny and me back at our normal jobs, I'm in a pretty good mood.

Besides, Jada sent me some ideas to defeat the next monster in *Sandbox XXL*—a colossal sea worm as big as a blue whale and with four rows of sharp teeth. Take it from me, level thirty-five is intense.

As I come into the house, I look down the

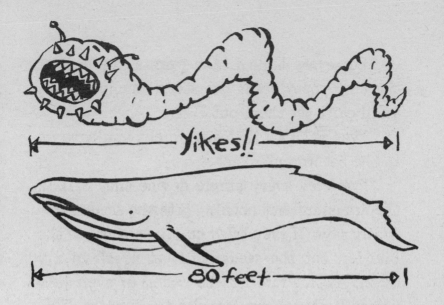

Yikes!!

80 feet

front hallway and spot Emily in the kitchen. As usual, she is wearing her GRUMPY FACE.

"You okay, Em?" I ask, feeling softer toward her after seeing all her supplies in the bathroom.

She points to a platter filled with poppy-seed bagels.

"Mom picked these up. Poppy-seed bagels are my favorite bagel," Emily says, shaking her head.

Apparently she's given up the no-talking thing completely. She continues.

"But every time I take even a single bite, the tiny poppy seeds get stuck in my braces, and I can't get them out."

"Even with all that equipment you have up in the bathroom?" I ask.

"I've tried every single device they sell in the drugstore, but nothing gets the seeds out," Emily says. "I even tried putting a bagel in the blender, but the seeds still get stuck in my teeth. At this rate it'll be *months* or even *years* before I can eat my favorite foods again. This is totally unfair!"

Is this perfect or what?

It's like I just walked into a commercial for the Candy Toothbrush!

I pull a new Candy Toothbrush prototype from my backpack, thankful I made a few extras. (We can't use the same prototypes on everyone—that would be gross!) I flip the switch from "no braces" to "braces."

"Eat your bagel, Em," I say. "Then go brush your teeth with this."

"What is it?" Emily asks, taking the

prototype from my hand. "It looks like a REG-ULAR TOOTHBRUSH."

"That's the beauty of it," I say, still sounding like I'm trying to sell it to store buyer. Hey, I guess some of the CFO stuff *did* rub off on me. "It only *looks* like a regular toothbrush, but it's not. It's Sure Things, Inc.'s latest invention, the Candy Toothbrush. It makes toothpaste taste like candy and comes with a setting for people with braces. It works even better than a regular toothbrush. You might even say, . . . it's a SURE THING!"

Emily scrunches up her face and gives me a weird look.

I admit, I do sound like a commercial.

Emily's look clearly says: *If this doesn't work, you are sooo gonna pay for it!*

As I go upstairs I see Emily cutting her poppy-seed bagel and heading toward the fridge for cream cheese.

In my room I stretch out on my bed and boot up *Sandbox XXL*. It's go time.

I try getting past level thirty-five three

times, but each time, I end up dying and have to use another life. How am I ever going to beat this level?!

I take out my phone and decide to text Jada. If anyone knows how to beat the giant sea worm, she will. Then I decide to check on Emily. She's not in the kitchen anymore, but I can hear the water running in the bathroom.

A few minutes later the bathroom door swings open. Emily grasps the Candy Toothbrush in her fist and waves it at me.

"It's too bad you already have a product called the Magical Microphone," she says, "Because this really is a MAGICAL TOOTHBRUSH!" She smiles, revealing a mouthful of teeth and braces that are completely clean!

Emily hugs me. Actually hugs me! Have we ever hugged before?!

"Not a single poppy seed anywhere in my braces and it really made the toothpaste taste like candy!" she practically shouts.

I breathe a sigh of relief.

"Nice to see you smile again, Em," I say.

"Don't get all mushy on me now, okay," she says. Then she ruffles my hair.

Big sisters. Who can figure them out?

The good news is that the Candy Toothbrush works on both settings—braces and no braces. And it makes toothpaste taste like candy. Sure Thing, Inc.'s Next Big Thing is ready to go! I have to tell Manny!

As I pick up my phone to text Manny, I see that Jada has texted me back. In all my excitement, I almost forgot about *Sandbox XXL!*

> Hey, Billy, I was going to ask you yesterday when we met at the dentist's office, but then that meeting got canceled and I didn't get to see you. Are you going with anyone to Petula's pool party? If not, would you be interested in going with me? Happy to tell you all about *Sandbox XXL* there!

I stare at my phone. Did Jada just ask me to go to the pool party? Sweet, funny, smart Jada?

Moreover, I can't believe how *happy* I am to be going with someone was awesome as her!

I text Jada back:

> I'd love to! Thanks! See you there . . . bring your tips for defeating this giant sea worm!

I'm going to the party! With Jada!

I arrive at Petula's house the next afternoon and head right to the backyard. The place is packed with kids—some are in the pool, some toss Frisbees around on the big lawn, and others set up a water slide.

I spot Allison Arnolds standing by herself. Hmm, that's weird. Why is she by herself? She asked Peter MacHale to come to the party, but I don't see Peter anywhere.

"Hi, Billy!" says a voice from behind me. It's Clayton Harris, followed by Samantha, of course.

"Hi, Clayton. Hi, Samantha," I say. "It's nice to see you. Looks like a fun party."

"I'm glad you came, Billy," says Samantha.
"Who asked you?"

"Well, actually–"

"I did!"

I turn around and see Jada.

"Jada!" I say, and give her a hug. I introduce
everyone quickly.

I see Allison walking toward us.

"Hey, Billy," Allison says.

"Hey Allison," I say, feeling so very happy
that Jada is the one who asked me here. "Peter
MacHale told me he was coming with you.
Where is he?"

Allison shakes her head and rolls her eyes.
"Up there," she says, pointing at the diving
board at the far end of the pool. I see Peter
standing on the edge of the diving board with
his arms spread open wide.

"Hey, everybody!" Peter shouts. "Cannon
baaaaaall!!!"

SPLASH!

He hits the water with a tremendous splash,
sending a wave out of the pool. Everyone who

was near the edge of the pool gets soaked.

Cries of, "Hey!" and "I'm all wet now!" and "You'll pay for this, Peter!" come from around the pool.

Allison shakes her head. "That's Peter," she says, annoyed. Then she heads over to join him in the pool. Clayton and Samantha also walk over to the water, leaving me alone with Jada for the first time.

"I'm really glad you asked me to come, Jada," I say. "I would've been sorry to miss this party."

"I'm surprised but glad no one else asked you first, Billy," Jada replies. "And I'm also really happy the way everything is working out with Sure Thing's Inc.'s newest invention."

"Did I hear somebody mention Sure Things, Inc.?" says a voice.

I look up, and it's Manny! He walks over to us with Petula.

"So glad you could be here, Billy," Petula says, as if she didn't devise this dumb invitation system. "Hey, Jada. It's cool to see my school friends and my foosball travel team friends hanging out together."

Huh. I guess I never even questioned why Jada even knew Petula to begin with, but I guess that makes sense. Jada and Nat don't go to Fillmore Middle School with the rest of us. Also, Jada plays travel foosball? She must be a master! How much cooler can she get?

"Well, enough chitchat," Petula says. "Who wants to eat?"

We follow Petula over to a long table filled with food.

I love party food—especially summer party food, like ice cream, smoothies, popsicles—but when I reach the table I get an unpleasant surprise.

"Check it out," Petula says. "We have detox health shakes, creamy kale salad, and, um, this meat plate here."

I stare at a platter with a mound of meat towering in the center. I'm not sure I know what color to call it. It's like the definition of mystery meat. Had I known what Petula would be serving, I would have brought enough Gross-to-Good Powder for everyone!

"What is all this stuff?" I ask Petula.

"My aunt took care of the food for the party," Petula explains. "She's very creative. Oh, and here's some cool news. She is going to be the new DIRECTOR OF CAFETERIA SERVICES at Fillmore Middle School this year! Pretty exciting, huh?"

I feel an uneasy grumbling in my stomach. I've had to eat my dad's cooking my whole life. I know what can go wrong when a bad cook gets creative in the kitchen.

Oh no . . .

If the new director of cafeteria services thinks this stuff is *party food*, what will we be eating at school?

Is eighth grade DOOMED?

Want more Billy Sure?
Sure you do!
Turn the page for a sneak peek
at the next book in the Billy Sure
Kid Entrepreneur series!

You know that first day of school feeling? That one where on the outside you seem calm and relaxed, but on the inside you're feeling a little nervous? Yeah, that feeling—the feeling that everything is about to change—that's how I felt last year.

My name is Billy Sure, and last year I became kind of a celebrity. If you haven't heard my name by now, I'm the CEO and inventor in charge of **SURE THINGS, INC.** I run the company along with my best friend Manny Reyes, who is our super smart CFO, businessperson, marketing person, and all-around numbers guy.

My life in the past year has been a pretty crazy ride. I've invented all kinds of things, like the CANDY TOOTHBRUSH, SIBLING SILENCER, CAT-DOG TRANSLATOR, and the ALL BALL. I also got to work on a secret mission for spies, be part of a few reality TV shows, and make friends with lots of cool celebrities!

So you'd think something as simple as the

first day of eighth grade wouldn't give me the first day of school jitters, right? WRONG. I may be starting eighth grade off right—with my best friends at my side, my invention company doing well, and texting a girl I kind of like—but deep down I'm just a regular kid who thinks the first day of school is plain SCARY!

"Don't forget," says Mr. Jennings, my new history teacher as he erases the whiteboard, "chapters one through four are due tomorrow."

Yikes! Homework? On the first day of school? Sounds like Emily was right—she said eighth grade would be harder than seventh, and I've already got tons of homework to do.

Emily is my older sister, by the way. She's a sophomore in high school now. I used to think high schoolers were cool . . . but now I don't even want to think about the amount of homework they get.

BRIIIIIIING!

The bell rings. As I hurry down the hall

to my next class—science—I get an incoming text from Jada Parikh. Remember when I said I'm texting a girl I kind of like? Okay, okay, that's Jada Parikh. Jada is also part of Sure Things, Inc.'s rival invention company, Definite Devices. I guess that should have made us enemies or something, but we are actually pretty good friends. Jada's amazing at video games and she's the number three *Sandbox XXL* player IN THE ENTIRE WORLD!

I open Jada's text. It's a picture of her winning a mini game in record time.

Scratch that.

NUMBER TWO PLAYER IN THE ENTIRE WORLD!

Jada doesn't go to my school, Fillmore Middle School. She goes to private school and they don't start their classes until next week. But we live pretty close to each other and know lots of the same people. She and Petula Brown are on the same foosball travel league, for example.

As I slip into science class, I notice that Ms. Soo has already placed a list of the labs we're expected to complete this quarter on the board.

No doubt about it. Eighth grade is no joke!

Ms. Soo outlines the way the year will go. Chemistry readings, lectures, labs. Biology experiments, films, field trips. A physics conference with the eighth grade advanced math class, demonstrating the connection between the two subjects.

My head is starting to SPIN. But at least she hasn't given us any homework on the first day of school.

"And here is your homework assignment for tonight," Ms. Soo says, as if my thought had jinxed it!

Rats. I add that assignment to my growing list labeled HOW IN THE WORLD WILL BILLY SURE GET ALL OF THIS DONE?!

BRIIIIIIING!

The bell rings again. As it does, I see Timothy Bu and Clayton Harris looking up at each other and shaking their heads. At least I'm not the only one surprised by all of this homework!

Next up is lunch. Thankfully, I won't have to worry about lunch—even eighth grade lunch. Not unless the cafeteria staff assigns me homework, anyway!

In the cafeteria I sit with a bunch of my friends at a long table. We're a pretty interesting group. Manny sits next to me. Around the rest of the table sits Petula Brown, Peter MacHale, Allison Arnolds, Timothy Bu, Samantha Jenkins, and Clayton Harris.

For a long time Manny and I tried to make it a point not to sit together at lunch. We spend so much time together at Sure Things, Inc. that we thought it would be a good idea to hang out with other friends at lunchtime. But now all of our friends like to hang out together. It's pretty GREAT, if I do say so myself!

I open the brown bag Dad packed for me. My dad likes to cook, though his food creations are a little . . . um, *creative*, I should say. In my brown bag I find one of his trademark PEANUT-BUTTER-AND-JELLY-STUFFED PICKLES. They actually taste better than they sound.

Like me, Manny brings his own lunch to school every day. He takes out a turkey sandwich in the shape of what can only be described as someone's foot. There are little pieces of cheese on what should be the foot's toenails. I guess that makes sense—Manny's mom, Dr. Reyes, is a podiatrist, and sometimes she takes her job a *little* too seriously. Or maybe she gets a KICK out of it?

The rest of our friends buy their lunch in the cafeteria. They sit with trays of food in front of them.

"How was everyone's summer?" I ask, a typical first-day-back-at-school question.

"I made some serious cash mowing lawns," says Peter. "I'm saving up to get a really awesome mountain bike. It will be the coooolest!"

If you ask Peter, everything he has or does is the "cooooolest!"

"I had a pretty good time at camp. Then I had to work at my family's fancy restaurant," Allison says. "I spent a lot of my summer saying stuff like, 'Would you like the elite set of silverware or the royal set of silverware, sir?'"

We all laugh.

Timothy pokes at whatever is on his tray. "I ran every day," he says. "This year I'm going to make the school track team. Did you know that it takes five hundred twenty-five steps to go around the track one time? I counted."

Oh yeah. Timothy's hobby is counting steps.

Told you I have some interesting friends.

"I worked with my mom this summer at *Right Next Door*," Samantha says cheerfully.

Right Next Door is our local online newspaper. Samantha's mom, Kathy Jenkins, is the main editor and staff writer. She isn't always factual, though. In fact, Kathy Jenkins has written some pretty nasty (untrue!) stuff about Manny and me.

"I was a lifeguard at the community pool," Petula says. "That's how I got this perfect tan!"

She holds out her arm so all of us can inspect what must be Petula's perfect tan.

"One time, while on the job, I jumped in after a dog leaped off the diving board!" Petula continues. "On second thought, maybe that was Peter!"

Everyone at the table laughs. Peter was a bit obnoxious at Petula's pool party this summer. He kept doing these MONSTER CANNONBALLS off the diving board and splashing everyone. The first time it was kinda funny, but by the fourth time it was, well, annoying.

"Ha-ha, very funny," Peter says. "But if you can't tell the difference between me and a dog—"

"Oh, I can tell," Petula says. "A dog spills less food on the floor when he eats!"

Again, everyone laughs.

"How about you, Clayton?" I ask. "What'd you do?

Clayton Harris is president of the Fillmore Middle School Inventors Club, a club I started. I was happy to hand it over to Clayton, though. Being a kid inventor and keeping up with schoolwork is hard—and it looks like it's going to get a lot harder.

"Well, Billy, I'm glad you asked," Clayton replies. "I started work on ten new inventions, which I hope to complete with the help of my fellow Inventors Club members."

"Ten! Wow!" I say, a little jealous that Clayton had a way more productive summer than I did.

"Yep, including a CHOCOLATE MILK LOCATOR, an AUTOMATIC TABLE CLEARER, and a HOMEWORK ORGANIZER," Clayton explains.

That last one sounds like something I could use right now!

As I eat my peanut-butter-and-jelly-stuffed

pickles, I glance around at the food on everyone's tray. Cafeteria food is notoriously bad no matter what school you go to (one of the reasons I like to bring to my own lunch every day—even if Dad does make it), but the stuff on everyone's plates today looks downright nasty.

Just as I'm about to ask what the weird-looking food is, Petula blurts out proudly:

"You know, my aunt is the new director of Cafeteria Services."

So she's the one responsible for serving up a plate full of something that looks like it just crawled out from under a rock. And now that Petula says it, I remember her mentioning it at her pool party. The food there was super . . . um, "creative"—detox health shakes, creamy kale salad, and some seriously mysterious mystery meat!

And now this!

"My aunt went to Fillmore when she was growing up," Petula continues. "She is *sooooo* cool! Look at what she did here. She used food coloring to make the chicken fingers match our school colors! How awesome is that?"

Wait. Hold up. CHICKEN FINGERS? Those gross green hunks of twisted stuff are supposed to be CHICKEN FINGERS?!

I don't know about your school, but at my school chicken fingers are the best cafeteria food we have. Why would anyone ruin Chicken Fingers Day? Everyone knows Chicken Fingers Day is the best day of the month! And these chicken fingers, they look, well, like . . . *fingers*.

Everyone has a pile of them on their trays, but as I eat my own lunch I notice that Petula is the only one actually eating them. The rest of my friends are working hard to eat the rest of the stuff on their plates—slowly sipping on cartons of milk, using their plastic spork to eat purple sorbet. I don't blame them.

But not Petula. Whether she actually likes

the way they taste or she's eating them out of loyalty to her aunt, she devours one chicken finger after another, until at last lunch is over.

BRIIIIIIING!

The bell rings and we all get up from the table.

"This was fun!" says Peter. "Wanna meet for ice cream after school?"

I think about all the homework I have on day one of the eighth grade. Then I think about the chocolate mint marshmallow cookie-dough swirl I could be eating instead. Magically, all thoughts about my homework DISAPPEAR.

"Sure," I say. "I'm in!"

Manny nods, followed by the rest of the gang. Even Petula, who seems to have survived her aunt's chicken fingers, agrees.

The rest of the day goes by smoothly, though I wonder if all the teachers got together and said, "Let's pull a practical joke on the kids and *all* give them a ton of homework on the first day!"

When the last bell of the day rings, I hop on my bike and head toward Jansen's Ice-Cream Shop, which is on my way home anyway. My friends and I squeeze in around a not-quite-big-enough table in the middle of the restaurant. I can barely see Manny over my triple scoop of chocolate mint marshmallow cookie-dough swirl.

We all start talking excitedly—this time about the new movie *Zombie Galaxy Battles*, which is coming out this week. Celebrity actress Gemma Weston is starring in it, but even though we're kind of friends, she won't give away any secrets.

"I heard someone is going to lose a hand in the new movie," Allison says, then cheerfully licks her strawberry shortcake ice cream.

"*A* hand? No way. I think someone will lose *two* hands," says Peter.

We jump right in. Everyone has their own theories.

Me? I don't really care. I'm just having a good time.

I shove another spoonful of delicious, chocolate-y ice cream into my mouth and notice that although I'm having a lot of fun, something is a LITTLE STRANGE here. I look around the table and realize what's strange is . . . Petula.

Petula has a scoop of ice cream in front of her, but she hasn't eaten a single bite. In fact, she looks a little green.

And Petula, who is one of the chattiest people I know (and that's a fact—I once timed her talking nonstop for a SOLID HOUR), has not said a single word.

"Are you okay, Petula?" I ask, wiping brown-and-white dribble from my chin.

"Hur," Petula grunts.

That's weird.

"How's your ice cream, Petula?" I ask.

"Hur." Another grunt.

The group resumes talking for an hour, until it's time to head home.

As everyone gathers their stuff, I pull Manny aside.

"Does Petula seem a little, I don't know, STRANGE?" I whisper to him.

Manny shrugs.

"She was fine at lunch—I'm sure everything is okay," he says. "She might just be stressed because of all of the homework. I know I am."

Manny? Stressed?

Okay, now I KNOW eighth grade is going to be hard.

DATE	ISSUED TO
1951	Matt Vezza
1977	Jada Reese
1696	Luis Ramirez

TIME MACHINES MAY BE HARD TO INVENT, BUT TIME
TRAVEL STORIES AREN"T! GO BACK IN TIME ON HILARIOUS
ADVENTURES WITH THE STUDENTS OF
SANDS MIDDLE SCHOOL IN

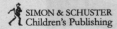

Did you LOVE reading this book?

Visit the Whyville...

Where you can:
- Discover great books!
- Meet new friends!
- Read exclusive sneak peeks and more!

Log on to visit now!
bookhive.whyville.net

Whyville

a Numedeon, Inc. property